Crush
Crazy

## Crush Crazy

Adapted by Lexi Ryals

Based on the series created by Pamela Eells O'Connell

Part One is based on the episode "Creepy Connie Comes a Callin'," written by Eric Schaar & David J. Booth

Part Two is based on the episode "The Trouble with Tessie," written by David J. Booth & Eric Schaar

**Disney PRESS**

New York • Los Angeles

Printed in the United States of America
First Edition
3 5 7 9 10 8 6 4 2
V475-2873-0-13350

Library of Congress Control Number: 2013936434
ISBN 978-1-4231-8374-7

For more Disney Press fun, visit www.disneybooks.com
Visit DisneyChannel.com

SUSTAINABLE
FORESTRY
INITIATIVE

Certified Chain of Custody
Promoting Sustainable Forestry

www.sfiprogram.org
SFI-01054
The SFI label applies to the text stock

# Part 1

Dear Diary,

Things are going so well with my job that I think I should get an award or something. Emma is busy with lots of extracurricular activities. Zuri finally started to do all of her homework and is getting good grades. Ravi is performing excellently at school, as usual. Luke has gotten really into break-dancing and wants to practice all of the time. The only problem is that Luke's grades have started to slip—I really need to find him a tutor, especially in math. But hey, one problem instead of one hundred is a serious improvement. I think I'll go see if I can find some good nanny competitions online—I would easily win!

Jessie

# Chapter 1

Jessie was sitting on a green bench in Central Park, enjoying the last of the autumn sun as she watched Luke break-dancing with two of his friends. She had to admit it—the kid had some serious moves. There were several clusters of middle school girls watching and letting out squeals as Luke executed a series of flips ending with splits.

"Careful!" Jessie called. "If you break your neck, your parents will break mine!"

A cute girl named Connie with long blond

hair plopped down next to Jessie. She had her smartphone out and was recording the dance routine.

"Doesn't Luke have the most amazing moves?" the girl asked her dreamily.

"Yeah. You should see how he wiggles out of doing chores," Jessie said, laughing.

The girl pulled a flip-cam out of her bag and held it up with her other hand to film Luke with both cameras.

"So why two cameras?" Jessie asked.

"I can't decide which is his best side," Connie explained matter-of-factly. "Plus, if I blink and miss something, I have two backups."

"Good thinking. Here I am—blinking and missing everything," Jessie said sarcastically, but the girl beamed at her, totally oblivious. "So . . . are you a friend of Luke's?"

"I wish!" the girl exclaimed. "I'm Connie. We're in the same math class."

"I'm Jessie, his nanny, and considering his grades, I'm stunned he even goes to math class."

"Oh, he does! I've got the video to prove it," Connie said fondly. "I've got Luke texting . . . throwing spitballs . . ." Connie smiled. "Going sleepy-bye . . ."

"I didn't know he could go sleepy-bye without Kenny the Koala!" Jessie mused. When she saw the odd look Connie was giving her, she hurried to cover. "Which is certainly not a stuffed bear he sleeps with, because that would be an inappropriate thing to reveal! The point is that Luke should be paying attention in math class!"

"You know," Connie said sweetly, "I'm an A-plus student. I could help Luke get his grades up. And do his chores."

"I love you!" Jessie exclaimed, hugging Connie. "Could you come over tomorrow and help Luke study?"

"Hmm. Let me check my schedule," Connie said, glancing at her phone. "Yes!"

Luke finished his solo dance to wild applause while standing on his head.

"Hey, Luke!" Jessie yelled over to him. "I got you a study buddy!"

Luke smiled broadly until he saw that Jessie was pointing at Connie, and then his look of delight turned to horror.

"Creepy Connie?" Luke asked as he fell over.

"He knows my name!" Connie exclaimed, obviously thrilled.

Dear Diary,

I can't believe I found Luke such a great tutor. Not only is Connie excellent at math and happy to help, but she's cute as a button, too! I'm not sure why Luke is being so weird about working with her—I mean . . . I know he doesn't love math, but you'd think studying with a nice girl would help motivate him. Maybe I'll make them some of my dad's famous kale and peanut butter bites for their study session. Nothing like a little brain food to clear the head!

Jessie

# Chapter 2

The next morning, over breakfast, Ravi was eager to show off his newest tablet app to Bertram.

"Bertram, check out this new fortune-telling app I downloaded," he announced, turning the screen so Bertram could get a good look. "It is called the Mystical iBall. It can see the future!"

The black screen was filled with a giant eyeball.

"I can do that, too," Bertram stated. "Listen: Am I done talking to Ravi about his stupid iBall app? Yes." He laughed. "Ooh . . . Spooky!"

"Please do not belittle my digital soothsayer," Ravi said seriously.

Just then Zuri came in holding three stuffed ponies. "Hey, Ravi, you wanna play Pony Princesses with me?"

"Mystical iBall," Ravi asked his tablet, giving it a shake, "should I play Pony Princesses with Zuri?"

"Ask again later," the iBall replied in an eerie voice.

"I am afraid I cannot commit at this time," Ravi said.

"I just need another Princess in Ponylandia! I'm not asking you to co-sign a loan!" Zuri said with a stomp of her foot.

"Stable your ponies and eat your breakfast," Bertram interrupted, setting two bowls of cereal and a carton of milk on the table.

"Mystical iBall, should we consume this cereal?" Ravi asked, shaking his tablet again.

"Signs point to no," the iBall announced.

Ravi shook his head and pushed his bowl away, but Zuri poured milk over her cereal. The milk splatted out in stinky clumps.

"Ewww! Chunky milk!" Zuri moaned.

"The Mystical iBall was right!" Ravi gasped. "That proves it can see the future!"

"No! It just proves Bertram is too lazy to go out and buy milk," Zuri said.

"I would, but it's so far," Bertram whined.

"The grocery store delivers!" Zuri exclaimed.

"I meant from here to the door," Bertram said.

❤ ❤ ❤

That afternoon, Jessie tidied up the living room while she waited for the kids to get home from school. She gathered up some of Zuri's dolls and Luke's Kenny the Koala bear just as Luke arrived home.

"Luke, doesn't Kenny the Koala belong on your bed?" Jessie asked him.

"Pft! No! What am I—five years old?" Luke replied, trying to play it cool. "I don't need that stupid bear anymore."

"Okay. Maybe it's time for him to hibernate," Jessie said, dropping Kenny into the wastebasket.

"Stop!" Luke yelled as he ran over and pulled Kenny from the trash. "Where's his little hat?" Then he tipped the wastebasket over, snatched Kenny's Australian bush hat, and placed it on the bear's head. "There you go, mate. No worries." Luke gave the stuffed bear a kiss.

"You might not want Connie to see that," Jessie said, shaking her head. "Frankly, I don't want to see that."

"I can't believe you invited Creepy Connie Thompson here to study with me. She's always checking me out," Luke complained.

"So?" Jessie laughed. "You're always checking *me* out."

"But when I do it, it's cute and endearing! Besides—hanging out with Connie will drop my coolness factor by at least eighty percent. That's like . . . half!"

"See?" Jessie replied. "This is why you need help with math. Now, Connie will be here in two hours . . ."

Just then, the elevator doors slid open with a ding and Connie walked into the room. Her long blond hair was tied up in a side ponytail. She had on a purple backpack and carried her math book and a binder.

"Make that two seconds," Jessie finished.

"Hi, Luke!" Connie said brightly, grinning as she stood as close to Luke as possible. "Sorry I'm early, but I just couldn't wait to see you!" She paused, catching herself. "Um, see you . . . get better at math. Which is why I'm here. Come on, Lukey!"

Meanwhile, in the kitchen, Ravi stood in front of Mr. Kipling and looked at the fortune-telling app on his tablet while Zuri sat at the table playing with her stuffed ponies.

"Mystical iBall! Is it safe to take Mr. Kipling for a walk?" Ravi tilted his tablet.

"The answer is . . . no," said the voice from the app.

Mr. Kipling flicked his tongue out.

Zuri looked up from her ponies. "Oh, don't listen to that stupid thing."

Ravi gasped. "You dare mock the Mystical iBall?!"

Zuri stood up. "I double-dog-dare! Give me that!" She walked over to Ravi and snatched the tablet from his hands. "I don't think you know anything," she told the Mystical iBall. "That's right—I'm calling you out, *iBall*," she said mockingly. "You gonna do something about it?" She rocked the tablet back and forth to get a reading.

"It is certain," said the Mystical iBall.

Ravi groaned. "Oh, no . . . I do not wish to be caught in the middle of your mystical smack-down!" He trembled and ran to hide behind one of the kitchen chairs, knocking one of Zuri's stuffed ponies onto the floor.

"See?" Zuri told Ravi. "Nothing happened."

Suddenly, there was the sound of ripping fabric. Mr. Kipling was chomping on Zuri's stuffed pony. Pony parts and bits of stuffing were all over the place.

"NO!" screamed Zuri. She fell to the floor and snatched the pony's tail from Mr. Kipling's mouth. "Let go!"

"That is what happens when you poke the iBall!" said Ravi.

Zuri clutched the pony's tail and shook her fists. "Why?!"

Ravi stooped beside her and put a hand on her back. "Do not worry, Zuri," he said. "You can get the rest of your pony when it comes out the other end!"

Zuri bonked Ravi on the head with the pony's tail.

Back in the living room, Connie grabbed Luke's hand and led him over to the couch as Jessie went into the kitchen to gather study snacks for them. Jessie quickly grabbed a tray of cheese and then stood in the kitchen doorway to spy on Luke and Connie as they started to study.

Connie sat down next to Luke on the couch and opened her math book.

"Let's try this one," she said. "Three 'X.'" She moved toward Luke. Luke scooted away from her. "Plus six." She moved closer toward Luke. Luke moved farther away from her. "Equals fifteen. Solve for 'X.'" Connie moved even closer toward Luke.

Luke scooted over a little too far and fell off the couch.

"Are you sure that's not a typo? Letters don't even belong in math," Luke protested as he stood up.

"Come on, Luke, you can do this. Think of it like . . . a dance routine," Connie explained. "Let's say you have fifteen moves in your routine and you do six solo moves. How many are left?"

"Nine. Not counting the encore my fans always demand," Luke answered confidently, hopping up and doing one of his signature spins.

Jessie ran into the room. "You did math!"

Luke opened his arms to give Jessie a big hug. Connie, excited, opened hers too, but Jessie set down her tray and caught Luke in a hug before Connie could get the chance.

"I knew you had it in you," Jessie continued. "You beautiful mind, you!"

"Whoa! If this is what I get for doing algebra, I can't wait for geometry. That's a math thing, too, right?" Luke smiled at her.

"A-hem," Connie interrupted, clearing her throat and glaring at Jessie. "We *are* trying to study."

"Sorry. You two little mathletes keep up the good work. I will *subtract* myself from the equation," Jessie said with a wink. She headed back toward the kitchen to watch them.

"So, Luke, I have another problem for you to solve," Connie said. "I need a date for the Harry Potter Costume Dance this Saturday."

Luke picked up the math book and started flipping through the pages. "I don't see that. What page are you on?"

Connie leaned over and slammed the book shut. "I'm not talking about math. I'm talking about chemistry."

"I don't take chemistry," Luke said, confused. "I'm not allowed back in the school lab since the explosion."

Jessie stepped into the room and said, "Connie, can I borrow Luke for a minute?" She laughed nervously and then dragged Luke toward the screening room.

"Sure!" said Connie, laughing. Once Jessie and Luke were out of sight, Connie got serious and began counting. "One Mississippi . . . Two Mississippi . . ."

"Can't you see Connie wants you to ask her to that dance?" Jessie whispered to Luke once they were in the screening room.

"What? Ewww."

"It's just one night!"

"I am not going to some stupid school dress-up dance with Creepy Connie!"

"She's not creepy. Plus, you should focus on girls your own age. If you keep hitting on me, I'm gonna start pulling my hair out!" Jessie said.

"Yikes. Bald is a deal-breaker," Luke said.

"Just do it because it's the right thing to do!" Jessie said sternly. "Now go be nice, or I'll rip your head off and play Quidditch with it!"

Then she turned Luke around and shoved him back into the living room before peeking through the curtains to watch.

When Connie saw Luke, she stopped grumbling and smiled sweetly.

"Hi, Connie," Luke said sullenly, shaking his head the entire time. "Would you like to go to that incredibly lame Harry—"

"Yes!!!" Connie exclaimed, nearly knocking Luke over as she hugged him. "This is so awesome! I already have our costumes picked out! I can't wait for everyone to see how cute we look together!" An idea struck Connie. "I've gotta go whittle you a wand!"

Connie grabbed her backpack and raced into the elevator, mumbling under her breath about different types of wands as Luke shook his head in disbelief.

Jessie walked into the room and looked pleased with how things turned out.

"She's whittling me something," Luke explained, glaring at Jessie. "And she has our outfits picked out. That's creepy with a capital K!"

"Okay," said Jessie, "we also need to get you a spelling tutor."

Dear Diary,

I'm glad Luke did the right thing—
asking Connie to the dance makes him
a real gentleman. And hopefully, he'll
see that while she might be a little ~~weird~~
~~odd~~ ~~strange~~ quirky, Connie is still a
good person who deserves to be treated
with kindness, especially since she's
helping Luke improve his math grade!
And he might find that he has fun with
someone outside of his usual friends
(that includes you, Kenny the Koala!)—
I mean, what wouldn't be magical about
a Harry Potter-themed dance? I kinda
wanna go myself. I would make a great
Hagrid. Maybe I'll call the school and
see if they need a chaperone!

Jessie

# Chapter 3

**B**ertram was making some spaghetti for dinner when Zuri and Ravi came in holding Ravi's tablet.

"Bertram, sit down," Ravi said solemnly.

"You don't have to tell me twice," Bertram said, dropping his spoon and sitting at the table.

"We have terrible news," Zuri told him.

"Your parents are adopting another kid?" Bertram exclaimed in horror, looking panicked.

"No!" Ravi reassured him. "But, the Mystical iBall predicts you will get hurt doing the splits, then you will choke on stuffing, and finally, a dark, shadowy figure will come to take you away at six twenty-two p.m. tomorrow."

Bertram shook his head in disbelief. "You figured all that out by just asking 'yes' or 'no' questions?"

"We asked a *lot* of questions!" Zuri explained.

"Hmmm," Bertram mused, standing up. "Here's a prediction for you: an incredibly handsome man is going to tap-dance out of the kitchen." Then he turned and tap-danced sideways out through the kitchen door with dinner forgotten on the stove.

Ravi turned and gave Zuri a nervous look. "The stench of doom permeates this room like a blinding fog."

Zuri fanned the air behind her sheepishly. "Um, sorry . . . that happens when I'm nervous."

Ravi wrinkled his nose in disgust and stepped back.

❤   ❤   ❤

Jessie was having a very good day, despite having to go out for emergency groceries after Bertram ruined dinner. She had convinced Luke to do something nice. He was learning lots about math, and so far none of the other kids had come to her with any problems that week. As she walked into the lobby, she saw Connie waiting by the elevator.

"Connie!" Jessie called out cheerfully. "So, how's Luke's wand coming? Are you going dragon heartstring or phoenix feather?"

"It's a surprise," Connie told her.

Jessie stepped onto the elevator. "Are you here to see Luke?" Jessie asked.

The elevator doors began to close.

"Actually," said Connie as she pushed the

elevator button so that the doors slid back open, "I came to see you."

"Oh, really?"

"I just want you to know that Luke and I are going to be very happy together," Connie said darkly.

"'Kay . . . ?"

The elevator doors began to close again. Connie pried the doors open with her hands.

Jessie knew Connie was a little different, but this seemed too weird—even for her.

"So from here on out, there is nothing between you and Luke!" Connie said with a smile.

"There *is* nothing between me and Luke," Jessie assured her.

"Remember that, because you do not want to make me angry," Connie said threateningly.

Then Connie reached into Jessie's grocery bag

and grabbed two oranges. She held them up to Jessie's face and squeezed them hard, squirting a shocked Jessie with orange juice. The juice ran down Jessie's face and jacket. Satisfied, Connie smirked and walked away as the elevator doors finally closed.

"Wow," Jessie sputtered. "Wand-making must give you really strong hands."

Dear Diary,

So it turns out that Connie may actually have earned the nickname "Creepy Connie." Attacking me with orange juice was pretty freaky. It's no wonder Luke's been so annoyed with me. I really shouldn't have forced him to not only hang out with Connie, but to also go to a school dance with her! Time to do some damage control—asap.

Jessie

# Chapter 4

As soon as Jessie stepped off of the elevator, still clutching her groceries and covered in orange juice, Luke confronted her.

"There you are," he said angrily, holding up his phone. "Creepy Connie texted me thirty-nine times today." His phone dinged loudly and he checked it.

"Make that forty." The phone dinged again. "Forty-one." It dinged again. "Forty-two."

"Yeah . . . Here's the thing about Connie," Jessie said, looking guilty. "We just had a little talk, and she might be kinda maybe a little . . ."

"The word you're looking for is *creepy*!" Luke shouted, interrupting her. "People get nicknames for a reason!"

"You know, in hindsight, maybe I shouldn't have pushed you into going to that dance with her." Jessie sighed.

"You think?!" he exclaimed. "Next stop: Dumpsville. Population: Connie."

"Okay, but just let her down easy. Tell her you have a scheduling conflict or something."

"Fine. But from now on, I pick out my own dates." Then he turned and winked at Jessie. "Speaking of which, my Saturday just opened up."

Jessie rolled her eyes. "Seriously, I will pull out my hair!"

❤ ❤ ❤

Later that afternoon, Luke saw his chance to get rid of Connie. He'd finished break-dance practice with his crew when he noticed her watching.

"That was awesome, Luke," Connie gushed, hurrying over. "Between your dancing and the Harry Potter theme, tomorrow night's going to be magical." She gave him an adoring look and batted her eyelashes at him.

"Yeah . . ." Luke said, squirming as he took a step back. "Speaking of magical, our date has disappeared."

He turned to leave, but Connie grabbed his shoulder and pulled him back—hard. Luke winced in pain.

"I will not be ignored, Luke," Connie said calmly.

"Can't think. Shoulder hurts!" Luke whined, trying to free himself from her grip.

Connie yanked down on his shirt with all her strength and ripped Luke's sleeve off.

"Ahhh!" Luke yelled, looking at her in terror. "Is my arm in there?"

"How dare you treat me this way!" Connie said, stepping toward him with a crazy look in her eyes. Luke took a step back, panicking.

"It's all Jessie's fault! She told me to tell you we had other plans."

"Jessie?" Connie asked in disbelief. "I told her to step off my man!"

"Well, she didn't listen," Luke said nervously, edging away as subtly as he could. "I'm sorry, Connie. I would say I'll see you in math class, but I'm pretty sure I'll be transferring into a different class, in a different school, in a different state." Then he turned and bolted toward the park exit.

Dear Diary,

Well, hopefully that's settled. Luke is going to let Connie down gently and I've learned my lesson. Next time Luke needs a tutor, I'll hire that nice old lady from the library to help him. Now, with that solved, I need to find out why I keep seeing Ravi and Zuri whispering over his tablet. They've been so well behaved lately. They must be up to something.

Jessie

# Chapter 5

**B**ertram had felt like he deserved a treat, so he made himself a nice banana split. All it needed now was some whipped cream. He shook the can and squirted a huge dollop on top.

"Ta-dah!" he announced, then accidentally squirted some whipped cream over his shoulder and onto the floor. "Oops. I'll get that later." Then he chuckled. "No, I won't."

Just as he dipped his spoon into the ice cream, Zuri and Ravi came in. Ravi was holding a plane ticket and Zuri was rolling a huge suitcase behind her. Trading cards were sticking out of the strained zipper.

"Bertram, Zuri and I will not stand by and watch you meet this terrible fate. You must flee," Ravi announced.

"We packed all your stuff, including your Famous Butlers in History trading cards," Zuri told him, gesturing to the suitcase.

Bertram jumped up and snatched out one of the trading cards. "Watch it! You're bending my mint condition Franz!"

"We are going to miss you, Bertram," Ravi said solemnly.

"What will we do without Mystery Meat Mondays?" Zuri said, looking like she was about to cry. "You always kept us guessing."

"For the last time, I'm not going anywhere!" Bertram said, flabbergasted, as he turned to walk toward his room. "Nothing bad is going to happen to me!"

Just then, Bertram slipped on the whipped cream on the floor. He tried to keep his balance, but his legs spread apart and he landed in a split. "Owww!" Bertram screamed.

Ravi and Zuri gasped as Ravi pointed to Bertram, and exclaimed, "The Mystical iBall said he would get hurt doing the splits! He is *doing* the splits!"

"And he was eating a banana split!" Zuri added.

"It is a double split!" Ravi said.

"Meanwhile, I'm splitting my pants!" Bertram howled.

Zuri and Ravi gasped again as they ran over to help Bertram up.

"A triple split!" Ravi amended, ominously. "The first prediction has come true! Next, you are going to choke on stuffing."

"And tomorrow at six twenty-two, a dark, shadowy figure will come to take you away!" Zuri said, looking frightened.

"Can it come earlier," Bertram said, wincing as he sat down, "and take me to the hospital?"

❤ ❤ ❤

That night, Jessie snuck into the kitchen for a snack. Thinking about all of the Connie drama had kept her tossing and turning.

"Oooh. Jackpot!" Jessie exclaimed as she pulled out a can of whipped cream, shook it, and sprayed it into her mouth. Unfortunately, nothing came out.

The elevator dinged, and Jessie walked into the living room to see who could be arriving at such a late hour. The elevator doors were open and lights were flickering inside, cutting through the dark, empty room. Jessie looked around, suddenly spooked. Rain pounded against the window and a flash of lightning lit up the terrace, revealing Connie holding up Kenny the Koala and grinning like a maniac.

"Ahhhhhhh!" Jessie screamed and jumped back. Then she rushed forward and locked the terrace door, but Connie was gone. Jessie squinted through the windows, trying to see through the rain. The terrace was empty.

Suddenly the elevator dinged again behind her. Jessie spun around to see the doors sliding closed.

"Okay, this is all just my imagination," Jessie said, trying to calm herself. "I did not see Creepy Connie holding Kenny on the terrace. This is all in my imagination." Then she noticed footprints on the carpet. "And I do not see wet footprints heading toward the elevator!"

Taking a deep breath, she stepped forward slowly. As she reached the elevator, the doors slid open with a ding. Jessie jumped back.

"Ahhhhh!" she shrieked. "Again."

There was nothing in the elevator except for a small white box sitting on the floor. A note was taped to the top. Jessie walked in and picked up the box. She opened the note.

"'Stay away from Luke, and let him go to the dance, or he'll never see Kenny the Koala again,'" Jessie read. She grimaced and then opened the box. Inside was Kenny the Koala's little Australian bush hat. "Poor Kenny! He's bear-napped and bareheaded!"

❤  ❤  ❤

The Kenny the Koala bear-napping was too much. Jessie decided she needed to put a stop to the madness and get Kenny back, so she arranged to meet Connie in the park. When Jessie arrived, Connie was on a bench. She was wearing her backpack as usual.

"Well, it's about time," Connie greeted her.

"Where's the bear?" Jessie demanded.

"He's safe," Connie said smugly. "Somewhere far away from here, where you'll never find him."

Jessie looked over Connie's shoulder and saw Kenny sticking out of her backpack. "Is he in your backpack?" she asked.

"Maybe," Connie said, trying not to let on that Jessie had it right. "So, is Luke coming to the dance with me?"

"Connie, you cannot charm a boy by breaking and entering, and stealing something he really cares about. I speak from personal experience."

"Luke told me you told him to cancel on me

40

because you had plans, but I'm telling you that's not happening! I'm Luke's girlfriend, not you!" Connie roared. Her eyes widened.

"What? I'm not his *girlfriend*; I'm his nanny!" Jessie exclaimed.

"Potato-potahto," Connie shot back.

"Noooo. Potato . . ." Jessie said slowly and then pointed to herself, ". . . nanny! Now give me the koala! It's time for him to go back home Down Under . . . Luke's comforter." Jessie grabbed Connie's backpack and pulled Kenny out by the leg, but Connie grabbed his head before Jessie could run away.

"No!" Connie screamed, yanking on the bear.

Jessie pulled back, and soon the two were playing tug-of-war with Kenny.

"Wow, I've seen bear traps give up easier!" Jessie said, straining to keep her grip.

Just then Kenny's head tore from his neck, leaving Jessie with his body and Connie with his head. They both gasped.

"Ooh! Luke's gonna be so mad at you!" Connie taunted.

"Me? This was your fault! Now give me back that koala's head!" Jessie said. "Huh. Never thought I'd say that," she said to herself.

"I'm keeping his head, and Luke!" Connie countered before running off through the park. "This isn't over!"

"I think Kenny would disagree!" Jessie called after her, holding up Kenny's body.

Dear Diary,

Creepy Connie just got upgraded to Terrifyingly Crazy Connie. Who steals a little boy's stuffed koala bear and then rips its head off? That girl is scary with a capital S. I have to do something to help Luke. Especially since I was the one who encouraged Luke to befriend Connie in the first place. . . . Oops. How was I to know she would end up being Team Voldemort?! Now I'm not sure Luke will even let me help once he sees what's happened to Kenny. Or how he'll sleep at night without him. Or, come to think of it, how I'll sleep at night knowing Creepy Connie got into our apartment so easily. . . .

Jessie

# Chapter 6

**R**avi and Zuri were determined to save Bertram from the iBall's premonitions, so they were removing all the bread in the apartment.

"We must protect Bertram," Ravi declared as he tossed out a bag of sourdough rolls.

"Okay, guys, I appreciate you monitoring my carb intake, but this is going too far," Bertram said as he walked in and found them.

"The next prediction is you're going to choke on stuffing," Zuri explained. "Then a shadowy figure's going to take you away for a permanent dirt nap!"

"So we are banishing all possible ingredients that make stuffing. Be gone, bread! Adios, eggs! Sayonara, sausage!" Ravi finished.

"If you keep tossing, I won't have anything to cook for breakfast," Bertram replied. Then he thought about it for a moment. "On second thought, keep tossing."

He turned and walked toward the living room, with Zuri and Ravi close behind him.

Just then, Jessie arrived home to find Luke sitting in the living room deleting voice mails from Connie.

"Hey, Luke, what's new?" she asked nervously, with Kenny's body hidden behind her back.

"Creepy Connie has gone from texting to calling. Could this get any worse?" he asked, shaking his phone.

"Maybe," said Jessie.

"I get it. I'm cute, I'm talented, and not to

mention I have killer freckles," Luke interrupted. "I was bound to have a crazed fan sooner or later, but we have to stop Connie before someone gets hurt!"

"I'm afraid it's too late for that," Jessie said, wincing as she pulled Kenny's headless body out from behind her back and handed it to Luke.

"Noooooo!!! Not Kenny!" Luke cried out. He didn't know what to do. He looked at Kenny's body and then threw the bear across the room.

Just then, Bertram, Zuri, and Ravi entered the room. "Don't be silly! I'm not about to choke on stuffing!" Bertram said to Zuri and Ravi. Kenny hit Bertram right in the face, filling his mouth with cotton stuffing. Bertram sputtered and coughed, pulling the cotton from his mouth and tongue. "Ew. Stuffing." Then he, Zuri, and Ravi all gasped. "Stuffing!"

"Next comes the dirt nap!" Zuri exclaimed in horror.

Bertram burst into tears and pulled Ravi and Zuri into a hug, while Luke ran to Kenny's body and cradled it in his arms.

"Kenny!" Luke cried.

"Okay, everyone calm down! Let's not lose our heads!" Jessie shouted over all of the crying. When Luke started crying harder, she grimaced. "Sorry. Bad choice of words."

Dear Diary,

I am in over my head. Zuri and Ravi are convinced Bertram is going to take a dirt nap. Luke is so upset about Kenny that he won't even talk to me. And I still don't know what to do about Creepy Connie. I have a feeling that she hasn't given up on dating Luke yet. I'm not sure what the next level of crazy is, but I'm pretty sure we're about to find out. What am I going to do?

Jessie

# Chapter 7

"**H**ey, buddy. I baked you some 'Sorry I set you up with Creepy Connie' cookies," Jessie said when she finally found Luke brooding out on the terrace. "They're extra nutty, like her."

"I'm not speaking to you," he replied. "Except for just then. And then. You know what I mean."

"Look, you did make Connie think we were dating, so we're kind of even, right?" Jessie asked, sitting down across from him.

"That depends. Did *your* best friend get decapitated today?"

"I said I was sorry."

"Don't apologize to me. Apologize to Kenny!" Luke snapped, holding up his headless bear. "Oh, that's right—he can't hear you because he doesn't have ears!"

❤  ❤  ❤

It was almost six twenty-two p.m. Bertram was more nervous than he'd ever been in his life, and Zuri and Ravi weren't helping.

"It's six twenty-one. One minute left," Zuri said, watching a small digital clock on the coffee table.

"Do not worry, Bertram! Any shadowy figure will have to go through me first," Ravi said, trying to make Bertram feel better.

"And I'll treasure those three extra seconds," Bertram said sarcastically. "This is ridiculous. There's no shadowy figure coming to take me away at six twenty-two. One minute later, I'll still be here with you guys. . . . Wow, this is a lose-lose situation."

"Suddenly, I don't feel so bad about looking for a new butler at six twenty-three," Zuri countered.

The clock's digits flipped to six twenty-two.

Nothing happened.

Everyone looked at each other in silence.

"I can't believe you guys got me all worked up for nothing!" Bertram finally said.

Just then the elevator doors opened with a loud ding, revealing a dark, shadowy figure. Then the elevator lights flickered and went out.

Bertram looked around for something to use to defend himself, but all he found was a feather duster.

"Bertram. You have company!" Ravi hissed, and then dove behind the couch for protection.

"Thanks a lot," Bertram mumbled.

Zuri stepped in front of him. "I got your back,

Bertram," she said and then called out, "You want a piece of this butler? Bring it!"

The cloaked figure stepped out of the elevator and raised a stick with something on it over its head.

Zuri's eyes grew wide and she squeaked, "I'm out. Holler at me from the other side." Then she dove behind the couch with Ravi.

"Please, please, please don't take me," Bertram pleaded. "Take the children! They're hiding behind the couch!"

Zuri and Ravi rolled their eyes. The figure reached up and pulled back its hood. It was Creepy Connie, and she was holding Kenny's head on the end of a stick. Her face was streaked with white and black makeup and she looked especially creepy in her long, black, hooded cloak.

"Ahhh! It's hideous!" Bertram screamed.

"It's just a kid," Zuri said, exasperated, as she and Ravi stood up.

"I know! Ahhhh!!" Bertram wailed.

Jessie and Luke came running in to see what all of the screaming was about. They both yelped when they saw Connie.

"Connie's dressed like the Grim Reaper. That is not a good sign," Jessie whispered to Luke.

"I'm not the Grim Reaper," Connie told them. "I am a Dementor!"

"More like demonic," Luke said under his breath.

"Ready to go to the dance, Luke?" Connie asked sweetly. "Kenny and I are. Right, Kenny?" Connie waved her stick, which was clearly a Harry Potter wand, and Kenny's head bobbed up and down.

"That's just wrong," Luke whimpered.

"Look, Creepy—I mean, Connie—trust me.

Luke is not the guy for you," Jessie said, stepping in between Connie and Luke.

"Yes, he is! Luke is perfect!" Connie snapped.

Jessie, Bertram, Ravi, and Zuri all burst into giggles at that statement.

"Hey!" Luke exclaimed, offended.

"Connie, do you really want to go out with a guy who still sleeps with a stuffed animal?" Jessie asked.

"And a night-light," Zuri added.

"It's a reading light!" Luke protested.

"Yeah," Zuri giggled. "Shaped like a choo-choo!"

"Luke also has the personal hygiene of a wolverine," Ravi said.

"That's an insult to wolverines," Bertram laughed.

Connie wrinkled her nose at that. "Eww.

Luke, is all this true?" she asked.

"Yep, and it's just the tip of a smelly, disgusting iceberg," Luke replied, seeing a possible way out.

Connie thought for a moment and then shrugged. "Who cares? When you really love someone, you can overlook anything."

"Oh. Then I guess you don't care that Luke hasn't read one word of any of the Harry Potter books?" Jessie asked.

Connie gasped.

"I haven't even seen the movies," Luke added.

Connie gasped and staggered back, looking horrified. Then she turned to leave. "So this is what it feels like when love dies," she said sadly as she tossed Kenny's head onto the ground and walked into the elevator.

The doors closed and everyone breathed a sigh of relief. Luke rushed to grab Kenny's head, and he held it against his body. "I can't believe you guys made me out to be so immature and revolting and illiterate," he said. Then he smiled. "You're the best!"

Jessie looked at Kenny and told Luke, "Get him on the table!"

Zuri, Ravi, Luke, and Bertram gathered around the table as they set down Kenny.

"I need a needle, thread, and 300 cc's of stuffing—stat!" Jessie demanded.

"Do you really think you can fix him?" Luke cried.

"Hey!" said Jessie, straightening up. "If I can fix Zuri's pony after it went through Mr. Kipling, I can fix anything."

Zuri thought about her pony. "Her tail is where her head used to be, but she can still run like the wind."

Dear Diary,

Well, all's well that ends well . . .

I guess. Bertram is back to his old

self. Ravi has sworn off the iBall and

is open to playing Pony Princesses

with Zuri whenever she asks. Luke

has vowed never to have anything to

do with ~~Harry Potter~~—ever. I sewed

Kenny's head back on, so Luke is

sleeping again. The one good thing

to come out of all of this is that we

have a fun new game we've been

playing: Zuri and I take turns calling

Luke and pretending to be Creepy

Connie. Listening to him scream is

pretty funny!

Jessie

# Part 2

Dear Diary,

Love is officially in the air. Things between Tony and me are amazing! We've been dating for a while now and I'm just . . . so . . . happy! Tony is funny and sweet and we have such a good time together. I've never had a relationship go quite so well. It almost seems too good to be true, you know? But it's not! We're totally on the same page, just taking things slow and enjoying every day together.

    You know, I'm getting so good at this whole love thing that maybe I should try to set Bertram up with someone. If he were happier, maybe his cooking would improve.

Jessie

Connie was thrilled to be Luke's math tutor.

Luke's biggest math problem was how to subtract
Connie from the equation!

Luke pulled Kenny the Koala from the trash.
"Where's his little hat?"

The mystical iBall predicted Bertram would
be taken away by a shadowy figure!

Jessie baked Luke some "Sorry I set you up with Creepy Connie" cookies.

Stuart was Zuri's *not-so* secret admirer.

Stuart invited himself to dinner with Zuri, Jessie, and Tony.

Ravi and Luke waged a prank war on Bertram and Emma.

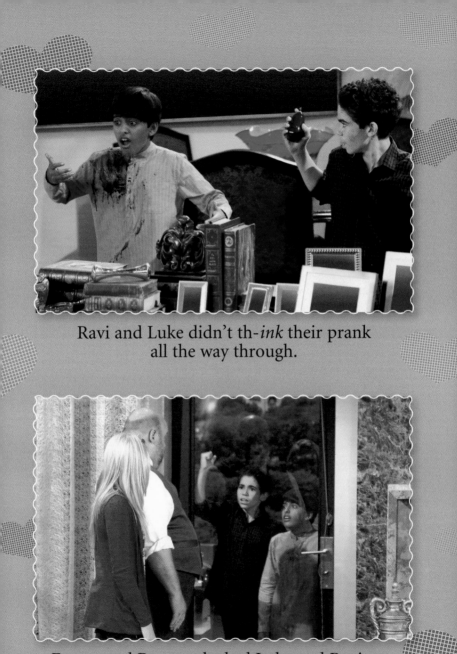

Ravi and Luke didn't th-*ink* their prank
all the way through.

Emma and Bertram locked Luke and Ravi out
on the icy terrace. Talk about *cold*!

Jessie was nervous that Tony would
propose to her!

Jessie tried not to panic when she met
Tony's parents.

The only ring Jessie was hoping to get at dinner was a *calamari* ring!

Jessie wanted to leave before Tony popped the question. Check, please!

Jessie and Zuri found Emma and Bertram
in a net—what a catch!

Zuri rescued a frozen Luke and Ravi
from the terrace.

# Chapter 1

It was a perfect winter morning, and Jessie was in the mood for an omelet, or maybe pancakes. She stumbled downstairs in her pajamas and headed toward the kitchen for a cup of coffee. She definitely needed some caffeine before making such an important decision.

"Good morning," a young boy said as she walked through the living room. He had dark hair and glasses and was wearing a tan blazer with freshly ironed plaid pants.

"Good morning," Jessie replied sleepily. Then

she stopped. There was definitely not supposed to be a young boy sitting on the sofa doing a crossword puzzle at seven o'clock in the morning. "Ummm . . . can I help you?" she asked, back-tracking to stand in front of him.

"That depends," he said, pushing his round glasses further up on the bridge of his nose. "Do you happen to know a five-letter word that means 'sorceress'?"

"Huh?"

"Uh . . . that's three letters," he said pointedly. "You're not very good at this."

"For a stranger who snuck into our penthouse at seven a.m., you're pretty judgmental," she said.

"I didn't sneak in! I live in the building," the boy said matter-of-factly. "Tony let me up. He said I looked trustworthy."

"Tony thinks the guy who sells solid-gold

watches for ten bucks is trustworthy," Jessie said.

"I'm Stuart Wooten." He shook hands with Jessie. "I'm in *love* with Zuri."

"Good luck with that," Jessie said sarcastically. Then she turned and called up the stairs. "Zuri, your friend's here to play!"

A few moments later, Zuri walked out to the top of the steps. She was still in her pajamas and her eyes were half shut. Stuart looked up at her in awe.

"Ah! The beautiful princess awakens from her slumber, brightening the earth and all who inhabit it!" he said.

Zuri took one look at him, scrunched up her nose, and stomped her foot. "Ewww!" she whined. Then she turned, trudged back into her bedroom, and slammed the door behind her.

"Witch!" Stuart shouted.

"Whoa," Jessie said, turning to him. "I'll admit Zuri isn't a morning person, but that's a little harsh."

"No, 'witch' is the crossword answer," Stuart corrected her. "A five-letter word for 'sorceress.'"

"Oh. I knew that."

"Did you?" Stuart asked smugly. "Really?"

"No. But I can drive," Jessie replied, sticking out her tongue at him. "So, nyah. Come on, Stuart, you can have breakfast with us and I'll get Zuri to come down and play."

♥   ♥   ♥

By the time Jessie was able to coax Zuri downstairs, Bertram had already made pancakes for everyone, and Emma, Luke, Ravi, and Stuart were eating at the kitchen table.

"I don't care if he annoys you! You need to be nice to him!" Jessie urged, pulling Zuri into the kitchen and steering her into the chair next to Stuart.

"Good morning, Zuri," Stuart said brightly, seemingly oblivious to the look of disgust on Zuri's face. "I was just speaking of our enchanting encounter in the lobby last week."

"All I said was that you had toilet paper stuck to your shoe," Zuri interjected.

"Yep! This guy's a catch," Luke snickered under his breath.

"Zuri, may your relationship be as comfortable and strong as the two-ply T.P. that stuck to Stuart's shoe!" Ravi said cheerfully, beaming at his sister.

"We're not in a relationship," Zuri insisted. "I'm *way* out of his league."

"Zuri!" Jessie exclaimed. "A girl never says something like that!" Jessie leaned in to whisper into Zuri's ear. "We think it, but we don't say it."

"No, she's right," Stuart said matter-of-factly. "But a guy can dream. And I do!" As he stared at Zuri, Stuart made his eyebrows go up and down.

"Aww, that's sweet," Jessie said, putting her hands on her hips and giving Zuri and Stuart a sappy look. "Stuart, why don't you come to the park with me and Zuri?"

Stuart jumped up, clearly ecstatic to even be included. "I'd love to! I'm gonna go get my playground pants," he said and then raced off to the elevator.

Zuri stood up and glared at Jessie. "I can't believe you did that. It's on you if someone 'accidentally' tumbles off the climbing wall." Then she stormed out of the room, leaving her pancakes behind.

Jessie laughed nervously. "You guys coming?" she asked the other kids desperately. "We may need witnesses."

"No can do," Luke said, shaking his head. "Ravi and I DVR'd Mixed Martial Arts Mania last night and we're going to watch it in the screening room."

"No, no, no, no. Not so fast!" Emma snapped. "Bertram and I are watching a *Couture Cooking* marathon in there."

"Huh," Jessie mused. "I never thought I'd hear the words 'Bertram' and 'marathon' in the same sentence. Guys, just figure out a way to share the screening room."

"Okay, we'll work out a good solution," Bertram assured her.

Jessie smiled and headed out. She was so glad there was another adult around to make sure

Emma, Luke, and Ravi played fair while she and Zuri went to the park.

But as soon as Jessie was gone, Bertram turned to Luke and Ravi and declared, "The big screen is ours!"

"But I want to see men get pummeled on a ninety-two-inch screen in HD!" Ravi groaned.

"And I want 'N Sync to do a reunion tour," Bertram said. "Tough." Then he reached over and gave Emma a high five.

Dear Diary,

Zuri has her very first boyfriend—it's so cute I almost can't stand it. I'm taking them on a little playdate to the park. I mean, I think he likes her A LOT more than she likes him, but maybe if they spend some time playing together, she'll come around. After all, he seems smart and sweet and he was doing the crossword puzzle in pen. She might not appreciate that now, but she will once she gets a little older!

Jessie

# Chapter 2

As Jessie and Zuri walked off the elevator, trailed by Stuart in his playground pants, Jessie spotted her boyfriend, Tony, the apartment building's doorman, at the front desk.

"Hey, Tony!" she exclaimed as she ran over to him.

"Hey, Jessie!" he said as they hugged.

Zuri stopped to wait for Jessie, and Stuart stood right next to Zuri with a goofy grin on his face.

"Give me some space, Stuart!" Zuri snapped at him, clearly annoyed. "I only need one shadow!"

"Your eyes sparkle like the ocean," Stuart said with a sigh.

"My eyes are brown," Zuri corrected him.

"Your eyes sparkle like . . ." he tried again, his face scrunched up as he thought. "The Hudson River!"

Zuri rolled her eyes and went over to stand next to Jessie.

"Guess what? I made us Tessie T-shirts," Tony announced.

"Who's Tessie?" Jessie asked.

"Us! Tony and Jessie," Tony explained. "That's what people are calling us."

"What people?" Zuri asked skeptically.

"Well, mostly just me," Tony admitted. He reached behind the front desk and pulled up a T-shirt, which he handed to Jessie. It read TESSIE! in big letters and featured a doctored picture of

Jessie's head on Tony's body and Tony's head on Jessie's body.

"Wow, these are great!" Jessie exclaimed, trying to sound enthusiastic. She pointed to Tony wearing her pearl necklace on the T-shirt. "And you are *rocking* those pearls."

"You gotta get me the name of your shirt guy," Stuart said to Tony, looking impressed. "I can see it now: Zoo-uart."

"Jessie, can I see your phone?" Tony asked. She handed it to him absentmindedly as she stared at the T-shirt, trying to figure out why her face looked so weird on it. "There's this great new app for couples like us." Tony pressed a few buttons and downloaded an app onto her phone. "This way I can track you wherever you go!"

Jessie blinked, clearly horrified. "Why don't you just put a chip in my neck?"

"Hey, Zuri," Stuart said eagerly, "can I see your phone for a—"

"No," Zuri exclaimed, cutting him off.

❤ ❤ ❤

Bertram and Emma were lounging in the screening room watching their favorite TV show, *Couture Cooking*. They had recorded the season finale the night before and they were ready for a marathon viewing session.

"I'm so excited!" Bertram said giddily. "Three straight hours of *Couture Cooking* and the finale is finally here!"

"Supermodels sassily sauté while they sashay and flambé," Emma said in a singsong voice before squealing with excitement. "Yay!"

She leaned back in the reclining chair and got comfortable just as Ravi and Luke stormed in and blocked the screen, arms crossed over their chests.

"That's it! It's our turn to watch Mixed Martial Arts Mania! Enough with your stupid cooking show," Luke said.

Emma scoffed and paused her show. "Natalia just cracked an egg on her designer shoe without breaking the yolk. If that's stupid, I don't wanna be smart."

"I doubt you'll ever have that problem," Luke said, rolling his eyes.

"All day we have avoided finding out who won the match so we could watch on the big screen like the gods intended!" Ravi said.

"We can't wait one more second to find out who won!" Luke said.

Emma sighed, pulled out her phone, and pressed a few buttons. She read something on the screen and then smiled smugly at her brothers. "Okay. 'Bone Crusher' Flanigan beat 'Skull

Smasher' Rodrigo with a tap out in the fifth round," she said sweetly.

Luke's mouth dropped open in horror and Ravi fell to his knees on the floor.

"Nooooooooo!!!!!" Ravi wailed.

"You ruined the match for us!" Luke screamed. Bertram stood up and held Luke back before he could tackle his big sister.

"Not nice, Emma," Bertram scolded her. Then he giggled. "Funny. But not nice."

Emma just smiled and pressed play on the remote control. She loved winning!

❤ ❤ ❤

It was a beautiful day in Central Park, but Jessie was having trouble enjoying it. She was a little preoccupied thinking about Tony's Tessie T-shirts and the couples app.

"Hey, Jessie," Tony shouted, breaking her train

of thought. "Check it out—I was able to find you because the app told me you went to the park." He was waving his phone around as he ran up to her bench.

"I told you I went to the park," Jessie said, laughing. "You didn't need the app."

"Yes. But I didn't remember," Tony said. "I've got something important to ask. Will you . . ." He looked back at the apartment building and saw a FedEx man walking up to the door. "Oh man, the delivery guy! Hold that thought," he called over his shoulder as he ran back to their building.

"*You* were the one with the thought. How can I hold *your* thought?" Jessie said to herself, shaking her head at her cute, silly boyfriend.

Just then, Zuri ran up and pulled on Jessie's sleeve. "I found out how to get away from Stuart," Zuri said. "By playing hide-and-seek."

Jessie stood up and spotted Stuart standing against a tree with his eyes closed. He was counting to one hundred.

"Now's our chance. Let's run!" Zuri exclaimed.

"We can't. I promised Stuart's parents I'd watch him. Besides, he knows where we live," Jessie explained gently.

"We'll find a new penthouse before he gets to a hundred," Zuri said matter-of-factly. "It's a buyer's market!"

As Zuri tried to drag Jessie down the sidewalk, they ran right into Tony. He was bright red and out of breath. He bent forward with his hands on his knees as he struggled to breathe. "Need to . . . ask you . . . a question," Tony gasped.

"Jeez, you're really out of breath," Jessie said, looking concerned. "The building's not that far."

"I want to ask if you would come to a special dinner at my family's Italian restaurant tomorrow night," Tony said once he'd had a moment to rest. "And you can meet my parents!"

At that, Jessie lost her breath and gasped for air. "Meet . . . your . . . parents?!" she exclaimed.

"Whoa! You're out of breath and you're just standing there? We should get a gym membership together," Tony said, smiling at her. "Gotta get back to work. See you tomorrow night!"

Tony headed back to work as Jessie sat down on the bench and tried her best to stop hyperventilating. Just then Stuart ran over and tagged Zuri.

"You're it!" Stuart said happily. "You didn't hide very well. You must have really wanted me to find you." He made his eyebrows go up and down.

"Stuart, I think we should have a little chat on top of the climbing wall," Zuri said a little too sweetly as she guided Stuart through the playground.

Jessie groaned and ran off to stop Zuri from pushing Stuart off the wall. It just wasn't her day.

Dear Diary,

I am in deep trouble. T-shirts? A cutesy couple nickname? A tracking app? Dinner at his family's restaurant? Meeting his parents? I'm not sure, but apparently Tony has gone from zero to sixty overnight and I'm just not ready. I don't want to break up, but I need him to slow down. Now how do I tell Tony that? I mean . . . . I think he ordered like a hundred of those terrible Tessie T-shirts. Why me?

Jessie

# Chapter 3

Jessie did not sleep well that night—she was way too stressed out about dinner with Tony's parents. After an early breakfast, she decided to spend some quality TV time in the screening room before the kids got up, but when she walked into the living room, she found a giant pink playhouse blocking her way.

"Hmmm," Jessie said. She walked over to the playhouse and knocked on its front door.

Zuri opened the door. "Howdy, neighbor!" she said cheerfully.

"Zuri, where did this come from?" Jessie asked.

"It was a gift from Stuart. I figure, for as much as he's bugging me, I might as well get a house out of it."

"Certainly trumps a Tessie T-shirt," Jessie said.

"You look like something's on your mind," Zuri said. "Let's chat in the kitchen."

"That'd be great," said Jessie, heading for the kitchen. Then she stopped and looked back at the playhouse. "Oh. You meant *your* kitchen." Jessie stepped into the playhouse.

"I made plastic scones."

"No, thanks. Bertram made breakfast, so I've already had rubbery eggs," Jessie sighed. She sat down in front of the little table and Zuri poured her a pretend cup of tea.

"Talk to me, sister," Zuri said.

"Tony's an amazing guy, but first there were the T-shirts, then the couples app, and now he wants me to meet his parents. I'm not ready to take such a big step," Jessie explained.

"You need to relax!" said Zuri. "So you're meeting Tony's parents. It's not like he's asking you to move in with him!"

Before Jessie could respond, the intercom buzzed and Tony's voice came through the speaker. "Hey, Jessie!" he asked. "Will you come with me to look at an apartment I found? I want to make sure you love it before I take that big step."

"I think. I'm gonna. Be sick," Jessie said, her face turning green.

"Not in the playhouse! Not in the playhouse!" Zuri yelled, trying to push Jessie out through the tiny front door.

Emma strutted around the kitchen, wearing a gorgeous red couture dress. Meanwhile, Bertram finished icing the most elegantly exquisite cake she had ever seen at the kitchen table.

"Well, it took us four whole hours, but we've re-created the winning cake from *Couture Cooking*," Bertram announced proudly, gazing at the dazzling blue and gold icing.

"It looks so good, I want to take a picture of it!" Emma squealed. "And then eat the picture!"

Bertram pulled out a knife and began to cut the cake as Luke and Ravi came in.

"Hey, we just wanted to say we totally forgive you for ruining the Mixed Martial Arts Mania fight," Luke said with a serious look on his face.

Ravi nodded. "Yes, looking back, shrieking that I wish I could feed you to our lizard . . . might have been a *slight* overreaction on my part."

"That's what you said in Hindi?" Emma asked. "I thought you were ordering takeout. No wonder the food's not here yet!"

"You might like to know we discovered a way to view the match," Ravi said.

"As long as you're not watching it in the screening room tonight. We have the premiere of *Runways and Ravioli*," Bertram informed them.

"Oh, no," Luke assured them. "We're watching it now. In the kitchen." Then he whistled, turned, and yelled into the living room. "Bone Crusher!"

"Skull Smasher!" Ravi hollered.

Two gigantic, mean-looking mixed martial arts fighters came in, flexing their muscles.

"Who are these guys?!" Emma asked, stepping back and wrinkling her nose.

"Duh," Luke explained. "Bone Crusher and Skull Smasher."

"They are being paid to recreate the bout that you spoiled for us," Ravi added.

"How much is your allowance?" Bertram asked in disbelief.

"The question you should be asking yourself is 'Where's my wallet?'" Luke corrected him. "Okay, guys. On your mark! Get set! Mix it up!"

Skull Smasher ran headfirst into Bone Crusher. Soon the two were grappling, knocking their boxing gloves together, and then putting each other into a headlock.

"Watch the cake! Watch the cake!" Bertram yelled.

"I sure hope nothing bad happens to it," Luke said with feigned concern.

"Yes, it is awful when something you care

about deeply is ruined," Ravi agreed.

Then the two boys turned to watch with glee as Bone Crusher grabbed Skull Smasher, picked him up, and threw him onto the table, crushing the cake. Chunks of icing and cake splattered everywhere, covering Emma's dress and Bertram's face.

"My cake!" Bertram wailed.

"My dress!" Emma screamed.

"Aww," Luke said sarcastically. "Poor you."

Ravi reached up and wiped icing from Emma's shoulder. He tasted it. "It is true what they say: Revenge is sweet."

❤ ❤ ❤

Jessie followed Tony up four flights of stairs and down a filthy hallway to the door of his new apartment. "Tony, are you sure you want to go through with this?" she asked. "I mean, I thought you loved living in your mom's scrapbooking room!" She wrinkled her nose as he unlocked the door.

"I've got to get out of there," he insisted. "This morning I woke up hot-glued to my pillow."

Tony finally got the door open and the two of them squeezed into a dark, tiny room. The walls were pale brown and the wooden floorboards were stained and peeling. A tiny kitchen lined one wall, and there was a toilet next to the sink. A fold-down bed took up most of the opposite wall and there were no windows in sight.

"Pretty great, huh?" Tony said with a huge grin on his face. "And only two thousand bucks a month."

"You'd think two thousand dollars would get you at least one window," Jessie said. Then she spotted a patch of black mold on the edge of the sink. "Or less mold spores."

"Oh, I got a window," Tony assured her. He walked over to the bed and pulled it down from the wall. The bed flopped toward the floor, but one of the legs caught on the toilet, so the bed just hung lopsidedly in the air. With the bed down, Jessie could see a small, grimy window above it.

"Ah, that really opens up the place," Jessie said. She didn't want to hurt his feelings, but she wanted to be honest and tell him the place was a dump. "Tony, your bed can't even go all the way down."

"The landlord said it's actually good to sleep with your feet elevated," Tony said cheerfully.

"And this neighborhood is so dangerous! On the way in, I saw three cockroaches assaulting a rat."

"Nah. It's family-friendly," Tony assured her. He pointed out the window. "See? Some kid drew a chalk outline of a man at the bottom of the air shaft."

Jessie cringed. "Um, I think that's a crime scene. Tony, this is a bad idea."

"No it's not. I've been thinking a lot about my future, and I'm ready to start the next phase of my life."

"You want to start the next phase of your life in a place where you can flip an egg from the toilet?" Jessie asked skeptically.

"Absolutely! That's gonna be a real time-saver in the morning!" Then he stopped and scratched his head. "Or is that gonna be weird when there are two people living here?"

"Two people?" Jessie asked, starting to hyperventilate again. "Isn't this place a little small? And the walls seem to be closing in." She ran to the door. "Can we go?"

"Yeah, we should probably start to get ready for dinner," Tony said. "I can't wait for you to meet my folks. Trust me, this is going to be a night to remember." He reached over to fold the bed back into place. As it slammed up against the wall, a thick chunk of plaster fell from the ceiling, leaving a gaping hole behind.

Tony looked up through the hole into the apartment above and waved. "Oh, hey! I'm your new neighbor," he called up as Jessie edged slowly out of the apartment.

Dear Diary,

Can you imagine two people living in that tiny, dirty apartment? I cannot move in with Tony. What's next? Marriage? ~~He~~ did say that tonight would be a night to remember. . . . Oh, no! I am not ready. What am I going to do? I keep thinking this will get better and instead it just keeps getting worse. I cannot go to that dinner. Maybe I can tell him I fell into a deep sleep and can't make it. Think he'd believe me?

Jessie

# Chapter 4

**Z**uri hummed to herself as she watered the plastic flowers in the window boxes of her playhouse. A gift like this house made it totally worth one afternoon of playing with Stuart in the park. She opened the door to go inside, and found herself face to face with Stuart himself.

"Aaahhh!" Zuri screamed, tossing her watering can in the air.

"Hi, honey." Stuart held out a single red rose. "Welcome home!"

"How did you get in here?" she demanded.

"I let him in," Luke called as he walked in from the kitchen.

Zuri slammed the door in Stuart's face and glared at Luke.

"Luke! You know I can't stand Stuart," she told her brother.

"I know. That's why I did it," Luke said with a smile as he headed upstairs.

Zuri marched back over to the playhouse and opened the door. Stuart was still waiting patiently behind it, with a huge grin on his face. "Stuart, get out! I don't want you here!"

"Sounds like someone needs a foot massage," Stuart said coaxingly. "I'll go get my oils." He winked.

Zuri sighed, slammed the playhouse door in Stuart's face again, and sat down on the sofa as the elevator doors opened and Jessie walked out.

She made a beeline for the sofa and fell onto it face-first.

"Men," Jessie groaned.

"Boys," Zuri said in agreement.

"Tell me about it," Jessie said, sitting up. "I'm pretty sure Tony wants me to move in with him. And, I'm meeting his parents tonight!"

"I know just how you feel," Zuri said sadly. "Stuart wants me to meet his turtles. And they're both named Zuri!"

"Plus, Tony said this would be 'a night to remember.'"

"Do you think he's gonna propose?" Zuri asked.

"Why wouldn't he?" Jessie said, throwing her hands in the air. "I mean, look at me. If only I weren't so charming and cute!"

"I share the same burden. Dimples are a

curse," Zuri said, folding her arms.

Jessie looked at Zuri and began to smile, an idea forming in her head. "Just in case, you're coming to dinner with me tonight," Jessie announced. "He'd never ask me to marry him with a little kid hanging around."

The playhouse door swung open and Stuart popped out. "Make that two little kids!" he exclaimed. "A double date is a great idea. Zuri and I need some couple friends." Stuart gave Zuri a hug.

"No we don't," said Zuri, slowly pushing Stuart off of her.

Stuart marched over to the elevator and pushed the button. "I have to go put on my dinner pants."

"He was here the whole time?" Jessie asked after the elevator doors closed.

"It's unbelievable, right?!" Zuri exclaimed. "I had an easier time getting rid of lice."

❤   ❤   ❤

That night, Emma was ready to get her revenge for the smashed cake incident. She and Bertram were out on the terrace, putting the finishing touches on their plan. As they walked back into the house, Bertram called out, "Boys, we've got something for you!"

Luke and Ravi walked cautiously into the living room, each with a swollen water balloon in hand.

"Whatever you have planned for us, just know we're armed," Luke said.

"Yes. I have a balloon filled with permanent ink, and I am not afraid to use it," Ravi agreed. At that moment, the balloon broke in his hand, drenching him in purple ink.

Luke doubled over with laughter. "Wrong target, but just as funny."

"Such pranksters," Emma said, rolling her eyes. "Look, Bertram and I are willing to give you first dibs on the screening room from now on, if you agree to stop messing with us."

"And give back my wallet," Bertram added.

"And what is the catch?" Ravi asked, dabbing ink from his shirt.

"You just have to sign a peace treaty that I've put out on the terrace," Bertram explained. "This prank war is just too exhausting."

"Never!" Luke yelled.

"I set up a buffet . . ." Bertram coaxed.

"Dude, why didn't you lead with that?" Luke said gleefully. He and Ravi ran out to the terrace to find a table loaded with covered trays. But as soon as they lifted one of the covers, Bertram slammed the door shut and locked it, trapping the boys outside. Emma gave him a high five.

"Hey, it's cold out here!" Luke yelled, pounding on the glass door frantically.

"And there's no food on these trays," Ravi added, after lifting the covers on all of the dishes.

"I built a fire, but that was mostly so you couldn't crawl back through," Bertram told them, gesturing to the double-sided fireplace that connected the terrace to the living room.

"How could you do this to us?" Ravi wailed. "Again."

"It was surprisingly easy," Emma said. "Now it's time for a model marathon."

She and Bertram laughed and then headed toward the screening room. But as they crossed the room, a net popped up from the floor, scooped Bertram and Emma up, and left them dangling five feet above the floor. Emma was smashed into the bottom of the net with Bertram practically sitting on top of her.

"What is—" Bertram yelled.

"Ow! You're crushing me!" Emma screamed.

"We knew you'd head for the screening room, right into our trap!" Luke laughed at them through the glass door. "Who's the best prankster now?"

"I think it is a tie," Ravi said, "because now there is no one to let us back in! I am freezing!"

"Me too, but the sight of Bertram's butt in Emma's face makes me feel all warm and fuzzy," Luke said, still laughing.

"Think how Emma's face feels," Ravi said with a snicker.

Dear Diary,

Okay, I feel a little better now that I have a plan. The plan is to bring Zuri and Stuart to dinner and keep them between myself and Tony and his family as much as possible. Then eat quickly and get the heck out of there— fast. I might try to look a little less awesome than usual, too, just to be on the safe side. And if that plan doesn't work, maybe I can join the witness protection program, since I won't want Tony's family coming after me if I end up turning down his proposal. Or maybe I can hide out in the screening room and watch sappy romantic comedies for the rest of my life. Who am I kidding? Bertram, Emma, Luke, and Ravi would never let that happen! Help!

Jessie

# Chapter 5

**T**hat evening, Jessie, Tony, Stuart, and Zuri arrived at Tony's family's Italian restaurant in Brooklyn. It was a cozy spot with red-checkered tablecloths, candles stuck in old wine bottles, and maps of Italy taped up on the walls. It looked like something out of a movie.

"Tony, this place is great!" Jessie exclaimed. "Very family-friendly. Not romantic at all."

"Tony, is that you?" Zuri pointed to a picture on the wall of a little boy wearing a uniform with a hat and opening the door for customers.

"Yep! This is where I got my start. I still have that hat," Tony said proudly. "Maybe someday I'll pass it on to my son."

At the mention of children, Jessie's face paled. "Okeydokey," she said nervously, pushing Zuri and Stuart forward. "Let's get our grub on!"

Just then, Tony's parents, Carmella and Angelo Chicolini, came over to greet them. They were followed by lots of Tony's other relatives, all of whom worked at the restaurant.

"There's my bambino!" Tony's mom exclaimed. She ran over and gave Tony a hug. Then she turned to Jessie. "And you must be Jessie. I'm Carmella. And this is my husband, Angelo. But when you're here, call us Mama and Papa. It'll be fun!"

Jessie's eyes grew wide as she tried not to panic. "Soooooooo fun!" she agreed in a high-pitched voice, trying her best to keep the nervous laughter from leaving her mouth.

"I hope you like hugs and kisses," Tony's dad said, wrapping her in a bear hug. "That's what you get at Chicolini's. We'd put them on the menu, but the health inspector won't let us."

"Understandable," Jessie muttered under her breath as he kissed her on the cheek.

All of Tony's relatives gathered around Jessie and gave her a hug. Seeing an opportunity, Stuart leaned in and hugged Zuri. She hit him with a bread stick from a nearby table.

"Ow!" Stuart said, rubbing his arm. Then he sighed dreamily. "Totally worth it."

As they all walked over to their table, Jessie noticed a series of pictures on the wall. In each picture, a different man was proposing to his delighted sweetheart.

"Those are all relatives," Tony said, pointing to the pictures. "It's a Chicolini family tradition to propose in this restaurant."

"Really!" Jessie said, looking uncomfortable. "My family has a tradition to never accept a proposal in an Italian restaurant."

"That's a weird coincidence," Tony said, completely oblivious to just how panicked Jessie was.

❤ ❤ ❤

Dinner was delicious, and there hadn't been any more talk of proposals or babies or anything serious. In fact, Tony's family had been really nice and fun. Jessie was finally starting to relax. The giant plate of pasta she'd eaten had probably helped calm her down, too.

"So, Jessie," Tony said, turning to look at her as he pushed his dish away. "I hope you'll help me decorate my new place. It's really important to me that you like it."

Jessie groaned. Just like that she was back to freaking out. Maybe she could keep Tony from talking long enough to escape before he asked her any other big questions.

"You know what I like? This calamari! It's dee-lish!" she exclaimed. She grabbed a handful from her plate and shoved the food into Tony's mouth. Then she stuffed some of it into her own mouth for good measure.

Tony's mother tapped her on the shoulder. She had brought Tony's grandmother over in her wheelchair. "Jessie, someone really wants to meet you. This is Tony's grandmother, Elda."

"Very nice to meet you," Jessie said, her mouth still full of calamari.

Tony's grandmother said something in Italian.

"Elda says you eat like a toddler, but she's willing to overlook it because you have excellent childbearing hips," Tony's mom translated.

"Check, please!" Jessie yelled, her eyes wide with fear. She lifted her arm to flag down the waiter.

"But we haven't had dessert yet," Tony told her, pushing her hand down.

"Can you all excuse us? Zuri and I need to use the ladies' room," Jessie said, desperate to get away from the table.

"But I don't have to go—" Zuri protested.

"Then come wash your hands," Jessie insisted. "You've been eating that greasy squid!"

"That was squid?!" Zuri exclaimed, horrified.

Jessie grabbed her arm and dragged her off to the back of the restaurant, out of earshot of Tony and his family. "Listen, Zuri. We have to get out of here before Tony has a chance to propose! Can you pretend to be sick?"

Zuri nodded. "Being out with Stuart, I won't need to pretend. I've been holding back my barf all night."

"Good. I might ask you to let it rip," Jessie said as they walked back to the group. But when they arrived, the table was covered in desserts. "Hey, guys, bad news. Zuri isn't feeling too—"

"Ooh! Tiramisu! Hand me a big-girl fork!" Zuri exclaimed, sitting down and pulling a plate of dessert toward her, Jessie's plan forgotten.

"Never mind," Jessie said through gritted teeth and sat down. She took a few bites of tiramisu herself. "All righty, everyone finish up your desserts. We really should be going before—" But Jessie forgot what she was saying as she looked down at her dessert. There, dangling from her fork, was a ring covered in custard. "No, no, no, no, no, no!" she muttered, panic truly setting it.

She dropped the fork, stood, and backed away from the table.

"Hey, where'd that ring come from?" Tony asked.

Jessie turned on Tony. "Oh, don't be coy!" she snapped. "Look, Tony, you're amazing, and I really like you, but if you think this is happening, you're a few meatballs short of a Chicolini Bottomless Spaghetti Plate!"

"What are you saying?" Tony asked.

Stuart tried to interrupt, "Maybe I can shed some light on—"

"Not now, Stuart!" Jessie said. Then she turned back to Tony. "What I'm saying is that although I'm extremely flattered, my answer is no. I cannot marry you, Tony."

"What?!" Tony exclaimed.

Stuart tried to interrupt again, "Jessie, I really think you want to hear—"

"Stuart!" Jessie snapped at him and then pointed at herself and Tony. "Grown-up talk!"

"But that's my ring!" Stuart yelled. Everyone at the table turned and looked at Stuart. "Zuri's ring, actually." He turned to Zuri. "It's a promise ring I got for you."

"Aww, Stuart," Zuri said. She took the ring and looked at it. It was beautiful. "Okay, I'll take the ring . . . but I'm not promising anything."

"So you agree to be my beloved?" Stuart asked eagerly. Zuri raised her eyebrows and kicked him under the table. "Or just a good friend. That's cool, too."

Tony started laughing. "You thought I was proposing?" he asked Jessie.

"Of course!" she said. "You wanted me to meet your parents."

"Sure! 'Cause I knew we could get a free meal!"

"And you wanted to share your apartment!" she continued, although she seemed less sure of herself as she said it out loud to him.

"Yeah! I mean, it's two thousand bucks a month!" Tony explained. "I'm gonna split it with my cousin Dominic. Not you!" Tony pointed to a big Italian guy across the room. Dominic waved at them.

Jessie waved back. "He has more square footage than your apartment," she said.

Tony sighed. "Look, Jessie, you're the greatest girl ever, but I don't want to get married for years and years and years and—"

"Oh! So let me get this straight," Jessie said, her voice getting louder as she got angrier. She had been relieved that Tony wasn't proposing right then, but that didn't mean she never wanted him to propose. "I'm just supposed to wait around wearing my Tessie T-shirt for years and years and years until you're ready to make a commitment?!"

Tony's mom shook her head. She could tell that this fight was spiraling out of control. "You're in deep lasagna now, bambino," she said.

At that, Jessie looked around and realized that everyone in the restaurant was watching them. "You guys heard all that?" she asked, blushing.

"All of Brooklyn heard it," Tony's mom said, pointing at Tony's grandmother who was holding up a video phone. "Elda's webcasting it."

Jessie's face turned beet red. She grabbed Zuri and Stuart and they ran out of the restaurant.

"Jessie!" Tony yelled. He jumped up and started to go after her.

"Tony, give her space," his mother said, stopping him from running out. "She's embarrassed right now, but she'll come around."

Dear Diary,

Well, that was a total train wreck. I misread the situation and acted like such a terrible girlfriend. First, I was so nervous about Tony proposing that I was really rude to his family. Then, when he acted like he'd never be ready to get married, I got so angry. I think I was just overly worked up—stress makes people do crazy things. I mean, it will be years before I'm ready to get married, too!

I'll be lucky if Tony ever wants to see me again. ~~Hopefully,~~ he'll accept my apology. Even if he does, though, there's still Grandma Elda's video of me screaming at Tony . . . Looks like I'm never going to live this one down!

Jessie

# Chapter 6

Jessie spent the whole elevator ride up to the penthouse banging her head against the wall. She was hoping the pain would knock the memory of that disastrous dinner right out of her head. Zuri patted her on the back, trying to comfort her.

"I still can't believe I did that. I can't imagine what Tony must be thinking," Jessie complained.

"He's probably thinking about how he's gonna get his cousin up four flights of stairs," Zuri said.

"I am having the worst night ever!" Jessie exclaimed. She couldn't remember ever being so embarrassed. She just wanted to crawl into bed and cry herself to sleep. But as she walked off the elevator and saw Bertram and Emma caught in a net and Luke and Ravi nearly frozen to the terrace door, her night didn't seem so bad anymore.

"Help us!" Bertram hollered.

"Let us in!" yelled Luke.

"Cut us down!" Emma demanded.

Jessie and Zuri turned and stared at each other in total disbelief.

"We can't take one night off, can we?" Zuri asked, shaking her head.

"You know what this means?" Jessie replied.

"We're surrounded by nitwits?"

"Yeeesss, but also . . . the screening room is free! I can finally watch that Channing Tatum movie!" Jessie exclaimed. Jessie spun and ran toward the screening room.

"Well, I think she's going to be just fine," Zuri said. She let Luke and Ravi inside and sat them in front of the fire to warm up. Then she got out her safety scissors from her craft supplies and began cutting Emma and Bertram down from the net.

"Zuri, hurry," Emma begged. "Bertram has horrible breath."

"Sit tight," Zuri told her. "Considering it takes me an hour to cut a piece of paper with these babies, this could take a while."

Dear Diary,

Well, the fallout from the dinner disaster wasn't as bad as I had expected. I sent Tony's family a box of "I'm sorry" cannoli from the best bakery in Little Italy and they forgave me. Then I apologized to Tony, and we had a long talk about our relationship. We're finally back on the same page—moving slow and having fun. He promised never to mention "Tessie" again and I promised not to delete the couples app so he can find me when he forgets where I am. And we both agreed that neither of us will be ready to move in together or get married anytime soon. And if that changes for some reason, we'll talk about it and make sure we're both prepared—no more surprises. I'm just so happy that we're still together.

Jessie

# The story continues!

Look for the next book in Disney's Jessie series!

# Livin'
# the Life

Adapted by Lexi Ryals

Based on the series created by Pamela Eells O'Connell

Part One is based on the episode "Somebunny's in Trouble," written by Pamela Eells O'Connell

Part Two is based on the episode "Teacher's Pest," written by Sally Lapiduss & Erin Dunlap

Dear Diary,

Everything has been going really well lately. Emma and Ravi have been spending more time together. Luke has been so invested in sports, he's been keeping out of trouble . . . for now.

   For the past few days I've been pretty busy with Zuri. After school, it takes every ounce of my energy to get her to stop talking about how much she wishes she could take home the pet bunny from her classroom. The girl won't give up! At least her class pet isn't a snake or something slimy. . . . Between our lizard and whatever's growing in Luke's room, we already have enough scaly things living in this penthouse!

Jessie

# Chapter 1

After school had let out for the day one crisp, breezy autumn afternoon, Jessie and Zuri strolled into the lobby of their apartment building. Glancing at Zuri's huge purple backpack, Jessie cringed, thinking that Zuri already had enough homework to last the two of them till December. Before Jessie and Zuri entered the elevator, Zuri stopped walking.

"Jessie," she said, "can I volunteer to bring Lucy, our class bunny rabbit, home for the weekend?"

"Zuri, when it comes to responsibility, you don't have a great track record," said Jessie. "Remember when you promised to start flossing regularly?"

"I floss my teeth!" Zuri retorted, putting down her backpack to point at her pearly whites.

"Really?" said Jessie, wrinkling her nose. "At your last cleaning, there was so much plaque the dentist fainted."

A smile broke across Zuri's face as she looked dreamily off into the distance. "He went down like a submarine," she said.

Suddenly, Zuri's backpack began hopping across the floor.

"Wow," said Jessie, pointing at it. "That is some hyperactive homework!" Jessie walked over and kneeled down to open the backpack. Inside was a white bunny rabbit with a few black spots.

"Hmm, that's interesting," said Jessie, scooping up the bunny. "I don't remember packing you a *bunny* for lunch!" Jessie stood up and saw that Zuri looked squeamish.

"I might have already volunteered. Oops," Zuri said nervously, recoiling.

"Zuri, the sewers are overflowing with all the fish you forgot to feed." Jessie covered the bunny's ears. "*And I don't think we can flush a bunny!*" she whispered.

"That won't happen this time. I promise!" said Zuri, clasping her hands together. "Please, please, please?" She tilted her head and opened her eyes, pleadingly.

"Wow," said Jessie. "Three pleases, the puppy dog eyes, and a head tilt." She spoke into the bunny's ear. "The begging trifecta!"

Zuri continued to pout.

"I don't stand a chance, do I?" Jessie asked her.

"Nope," said Zuri. "Give in or I'll close with the lip quiver." Her bottom lip trembled. "And a single tear," she said.

"Fine. I give," said Jessie, handing the bunny to Zuri.

Zuri smiled.

Jessie put her hands on her hips. "Next time I negotiate with you, I'm wearing a blindfold and headphones."

Zuri giggled as Jessie patted the bunny playfully on the head.